the GiaNT who played CHeCKeRS

By: Christopher Shirley

Illustrations By: Brian Martin

Once upon a time, there was a Little Boy who loved to play checkers.

He would go over to his friend's house to play checkers all day long.

Every day that he did,
he got better and better at it.

Until one day, the Little Boy got lost on his way home and it started to rain.

The Little Boy looked and looked for shelter, until he found a cave.

Little did the Little Boy know, this cave was home to a mean old giant named George.

The Little Boy sat down with his checkerboard
at the opening of the cave, trying to dry off.

Until a loud stomping
was heard and out
came the giant
named George.

"WHO COMES INTO MY CAVE?"
the giant yelled.

He was a true giant, tall
as a tree and wide as a house.

"I-I did, Sir,"
said the Little Boy.

"M-my name is Tim,"
he said.

The giant scratched his head as he swung his mightly club onto his shoulder.

"WHY YOU COME HERE? ALL OTHER LITTLE PEOPLE WANT TO HURT GEORGE. YOU WANT TO HURT GEORGE TOO?"

The giant suddenly became angry, getting his club ready to swing.

"No, no, nothing like that, George!" exclaimed Tim.

"I would just like to play a game of checkers!" Tim smiled, holding up his checkerboard for the giant to see.

Spilling a bag of little wooden pieces onto the board, he put them where they needed to go.

George the giant sat down in front of the board staring with confusion.

George the giant tried to move
a piece with his big, giant hand.
When he saw that he had
moved the piece, he laughed
a loud laugh
and clapped happily.

"HAHAHAHAHA!
I LIKE THIS
CHECK-KERS!"
he yelled.

The boy packed up his things and gave a wave to the giant as he walked out of the cave.

The giant waved back. For once, he found something that had made him happy.

Over the next weeks, the boy would return to the giant's cave, teaching him how to get better at checkers.

Week after week, month after month, the giant noticed that the little boy had been getting bigger, and had been coming less often.

Until it seemed that he never came at all.

The giant got sad, missing his best friend. He tried playing checkers with the mice who lived in his cave, but they never played right.

But one day, two little people came to the giant's cave, one taller than the other one.

The giant knew who this tall little one was.

It was Tim, all grown up into a big little one.

"Hi George," said Tim, "This is my son, Jim."

"HI JIM. HI TIM," the giant said, smiling, as he was happy to see Tim again. "DOES JIM LIKE CHECKERS?"

The littler little one nodded, holding up his father's checkerboard.

And so they played and played, laughing, cheering, and having a great time together. For weeks and months to come, the littler boy would play with George the Giant, until he too, brought a littler boy to play with him.

THE END

CPSIA information can be obtained
at www.ICGtesting.com
Printed in the USA
LVHW051926280719
625547LV00002B/2/P

9 781946 629166